A Friend for
DRAGON

Read more DRAGON books!

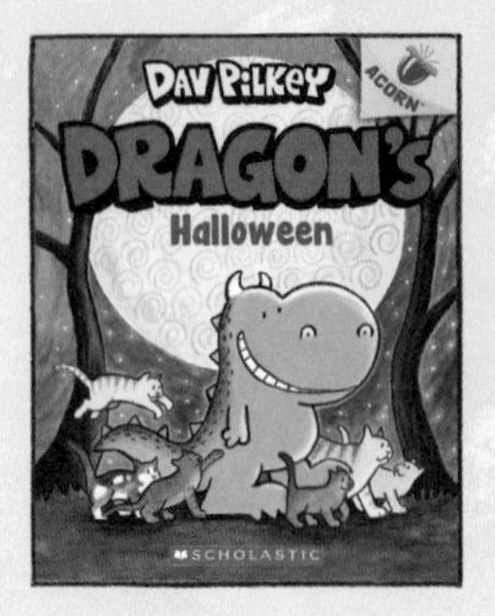

A Friend for DRAGON

Dav Pilkey

ACORN™
SCHOLASTIC INC.

Library of Congress Cataloging-in-Publication Data

Names: Pilkey, Dav, 1966– author, illustrator.
Title: A Friend for Dragon / Dav Pilkey.
Description: [New edition] | New York : Acorn/Scholastic Inc., 2019. | Originally published in 1991 by Orchard Books. | Summary: Dragon is lonely so he goes looking for a friend and when an apple falls on his head he is convinced that he has found one; but at home Apple is quiet and unresponsive, and when a visit to the doctor only makes things worse, Dragon mourns the loss of his friend — until an apple tree grows where Apple is buried.
Identifiers: LCCN 2018025743| ISBN 9781338341065 (hc : alk. paper) | ISBN 9781338341058 (pb : alk. paper)
Subjects: LCSH: Dragons — Juvenile fiction. | Apples — Juvenile fiction. | Loneliness — Juvenile fiction. | Friendship — Juvenile fiction. | CYAC: Dragons — Fiction. | Apples — Fiction. | Loneliness — Fiction. | Friendship — Fiction.
Classification: LCC PZ7.P63123 Fr 2019 | DDC [E] — dc23
LC record available at https://lccn.loc.gov/2018025743

10 9 8 7 6 5 4 3 2 1 19 20 21 22 23

Printed in China 62
This edition first printing, May 2019
Book design by Dav Pilkey and Kirk Benshoff

Contents

1
A Friend for Dragon

There once was a blue dragon
who lived in a little house
all by himself.
Sometimes Dragon got lonely.

"I wish I had a friend," said Dragon.
So he went out into the world
to look for a friend.

Dragon went to the woods
and met a small black squirrel.

"Will you be my friend?"
said Dragon.

"No," said the squirrel.
"I'm too busy."

Dragon went to the riverbank
and met a fat gray hippo.

"Will you be my friend?"
said Dragon.

"No," said the hippo.
"I'm too tired."

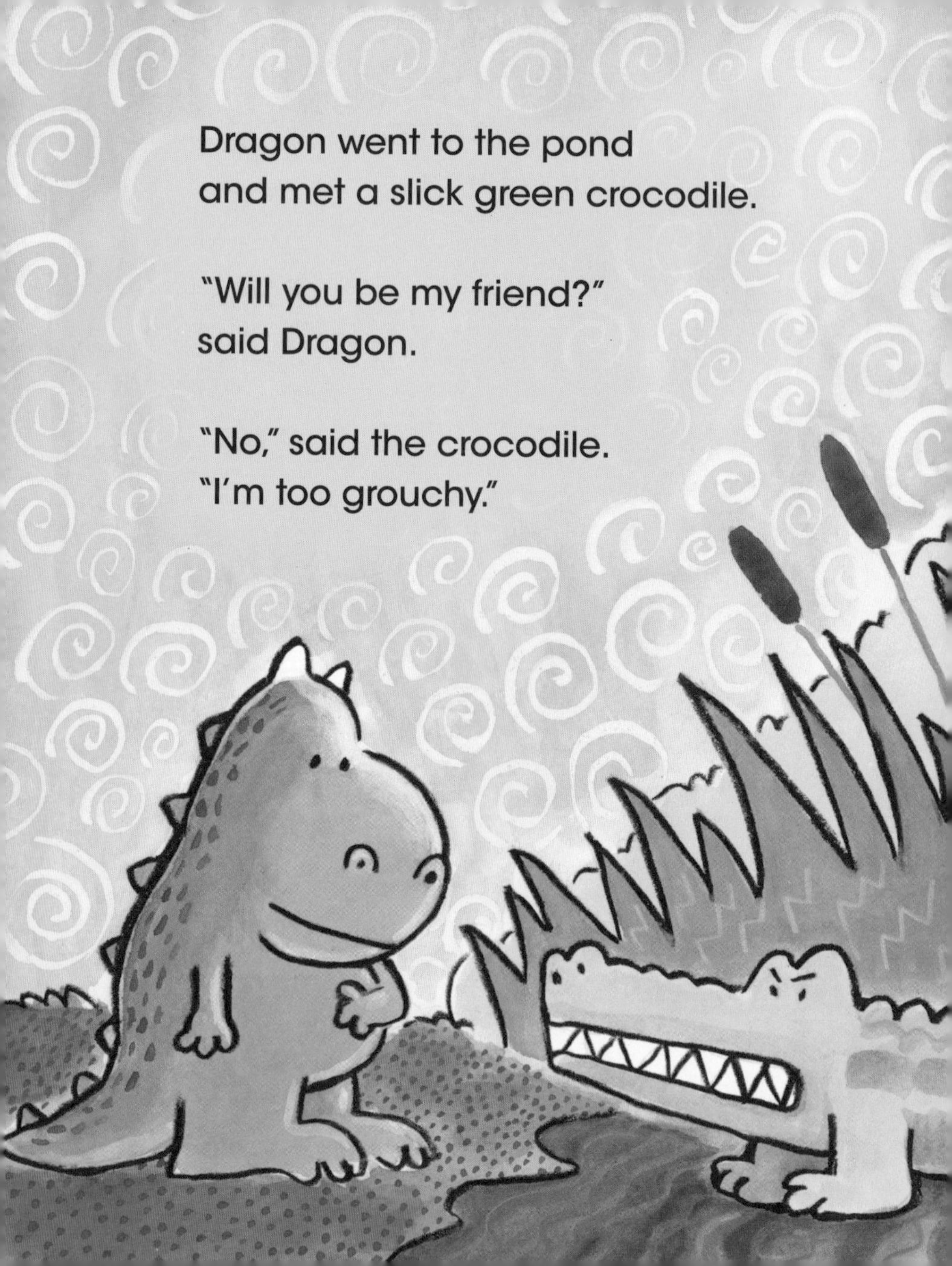

Dragon went to the pond
and met a slick green crocodile.

"Will you be my friend?"
said Dragon.

"No," said the crocodile.
"I'm too grouchy."

So Dragon sat down under a tree,
still wishing for a friend.

Suddenly, an apple fell out
of the tree and hit Dragon
on the head.

Just then, a little green snake
slithered by.
The snake wanted to
play a joke on Dragon.
So it hid behind a rock
and called out, "Hi, Dragon."

Dragon looked all around,
but he didn't see anyone.
"Who said that?" cried Dragon.

"I did," said the snake.

Dragon looked all around again,
but he still didn't see anyone.

"Where are you?" said Dragon.

"I'm right here in your hand," said the snake.

Dragon looked at the apple in his hand and scratched his big head.

"I did not know apples could talk," said Dragon.

"Oh, but we can," said the snake in the grass.

"Would you like to be my friend?"
Dragon asked the apple.

"Oh, yes," laughed the snake.

"At last," said Dragon.
"A friend."

2
Friends at Home

Dragon took the apple home
and built a warm, cozy fire.

He told spooky stories to the apple.
He told funny jokes to the apple.
Dragon talked all day long
and into the night.

"You are a good listener,"
said Dragon.
"Good friends are always
good listeners."

Dragon fixed a midnight snack.
He mixed cookies, orange juice,
and catsup all together in a big bowl.

Dragon scooped some of the food
onto his plate.
Then he scooped some food onto
the apple's plate.

"Just say 'When,'" said Dragon.
The apple did not say "When."

So Dragon scooped some more food
onto the apple's plate.

"Just say 'When,'" Dragon said.
The apple still did not say "When."

So Dragon scooped the rest of the food
onto the apple's plate.

"I am glad that we both like to eat
so much," said Dragon.
"Good friends should always have
a lot in common."

Dragon ate up all of his food.
The apple did not eat any food at all.

Dragon was still hungry.
He looked at the apple's plate
and drooled.

"Do you mind if I eat some
of your food?" asked Dragon.

The apple did not seem to mind.

So Dragon ate up all of the apple's food too.

"You are a good friend," said Dragon. "Good friends always share."

3
The New Day

The next morning, Dragon awoke with the sun.

"Good morning, Apple," said Dragon. The apple did not answer.

So Dragon went out to the kitchen and made breakfast.

When he was finished eating,
he tried to wake the apple up again.

"Good morning, Apple," he cried.
The apple still did not answer.

So Dragon went outside
for a walk along the riverbank.

When he came back,
he tried to wake the apple up again.

"GOOD MORNING, APPLE!" he screamed.
The apple still did not answer.

Dragon was very worried.
He called the doctor.

"My apple won't talk to me,"
said Dragon.

"Maybe it's a crab apple,"
said the doctor.

"No," said Dragon.
"I think it is sick."

So Dragon took the apple
to the doctor's office.
They sat down next to a big walrus.

"What's the matter with you?"
asked the walrus.

"It's my apple," said Dragon.
"It won't talk to me."

The walrus stared at the apple
and drooled.

Dragon needed a drink of water.
"Will you watch my apple for me?"
Dragon asked the walrus.

"Sure," said the walrus,
licking her lips.

When Dragon came back,
the apple had changed.
It was not round anymore.
It was not shiny anymore.
It was not red anymore.
Now it was wet and skinny and white.

"What happened to you?" cried Dragon.
"Are you all right?"

The little white thing did not answer.

Dragon wrapped his friend
in a piece of paper
and carried it home.

"Don't worry," said Dragon.
"Everything will be OK."

When Dragon got home,
the little white thing had turned all
mushy and brown.

"Are you hurt?" asked Dragon.
The mushy brown thing did not answer.

"Are you sick?" asked Dragon.
But there was no answer.

"Are you dead?" asked Dragon.
Still, there was no answer.

Dragon scratched his big head
and started to cry.

4
Good-bye

The next morning,
Dragon went out into his backyard
and dug a hole.

He put his friend into the hole
and covered it over with dirt.

Dragon made a sign.
On the sign, he wrote the word
"Friend."

FRIEND

Dragon was very sad.
He cried every day.
He did not want to eat.
He could not get to sleep.
Dragon did not leave his house
for a long, long time.

But after a while,
Dragon stopped being so sad.
He cried less and less.
He began to eat and sleep better.

Still, he was very lonely.

5
Summertime

One day, many months later,
Dragon walked out into his backyard.
He was still feeling lonely.
Dragon sat down under the big tree
growing in his yard.
He wished for a friend.

Suddenly, something fell
out of the tree and hit Dragon
on the head.

It was an apple.

Then Dragon looked up, and smiled.

About the Author

DAV PILKEY is the creator of the bestselling Dog Man and Captain Underpants series. He has written and illustrated many other books for young readers, including the Dumb Bunnies series, *The Hallo-Wiener, Dog Breath,* and *The Paperboy,* which is a Caldecott Honor book. Dav lives in the Pacific Northwest with his wife.

YOU CAN DRAW DRAGON!

1 Draw a backward letter "C."

2 Draw the top of Dragon's head and the back of his neck.

3 Put a smile on his face.

4 Add his eyes and nose.

5 Add horns on top of his head.

6 Draw Dragon's arm. He's waving at you!

7 Add his tummy and other arm.

8 Draw his tail.

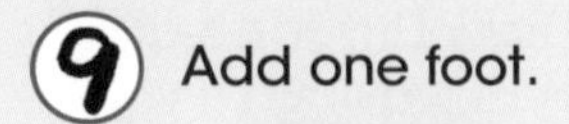

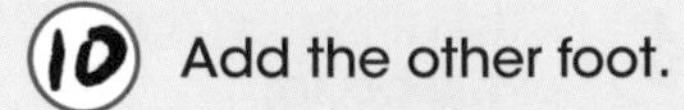

11 Draw spikes down his back and on his tail.

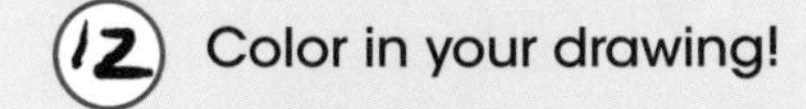

YOU CAN DRAW APPLE!

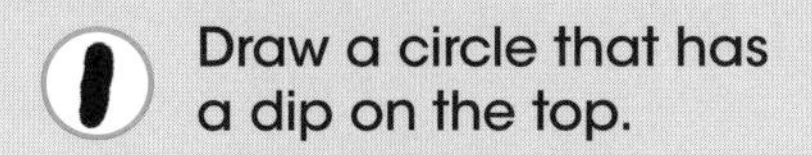
1 Draw a circle that has a dip on the top.

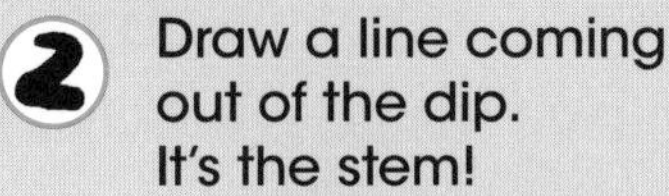
2 Draw a line coming out of the dip. It's the stem!

3 Add a leaf to the stem.

4 Color in your drawing!

WHAT'S YOUR STORY?

Dragon and his new friend have fun together.
Imagine **you** and Dragon are friends.
What would you do for fun?
What snack would you make?
Write and draw your story!

BONUS!

Try making your story just like Dav — with watercolors! Did you know that Dav taught himself how to watercolor when he was making this book? He went to the supermarket, bought a children's watercolor set, and used it to paint all the Dragon books.

scholastic.com/acorn